A DAY IN SARGENT SMITH

A COMMON MAN

DAVID LEE HENLEY

Authors' Note: This is a work of fiction. Names, characters, places, and incidents are a product of the author's imagination. Locales and public names are sometimes used for atmospheric purposes. Any resemblance to actual people, living or dead, or to businesses, companies, events, institutions, or locales is completely coincidental.

PREFACE

Do you ever get the feeling you're being watched? That eerie raises the hair on your neck kind of creepy, unnerving feeling? This story just possibly might have an explanation for that.

It might not be as ominous as you thought. Well, in this case, it isn't anyway. It is simply some unknown to us entities doing research. It is still weird though that we haven't been privy to any knowledge of their existence.

What form of life are they? Are they like us in form and intelligence? Are they a different species from a different world or dimension?

How long have they been around watching and hiding from us? What is there purpose in our lives? At this time all is a puzzle. Maybe at some other point in history, all will be revealed. It seems for the moment of this story though, now is not the time.

So, as we don't know anything is even happening it is certainly something to not worry about. Even if we knew about something to worry about. Confusing enough already isn't it?

So just relax and enjoy the story. There is plenty of time to ponder later as to who they are.

INTRODUCTION

Sargent Smith is a common ordinary individual that has been selected by a dedicated investigative body of which is unknown to humans at this point. It is obvious that no malus is aimed at us or Sargent Smith.

It seems we have an unseen force behind the scenes directing some sort of surveillance operation on the world apparently to gain knowledge as to our behaviors. It is also obvious these beings as we will call them are not willing to inform humans of their presence. At least for now. They are doing things on a rather large and broad scale.

It is only coming to our attention now because someone decided to write this short story about it. We don't know if this story is true or just a fabrication of this someone's imagination. We may never know.

All we have the power to do is read the story and wonder. Maybe throw a laser light toward a star at night and see if it winks back. Who knows what is real or not real anymore? Maybe imagination is just another form of reality.

A SHORT STORY

ORDER: This council is now in session. Order.

It has come to our attention this subject long thought about, but has never been acted upon has finally found it's time. We the council have decreed this matter be looked at so it can finally be put to rest.

You have studied the issue at hand from the documents we have furnished you?

"Yes," we answered.

The council has authorized funds for this project and wish to hire your research team to address this issue. We see from your prior reports; you have been very thorough in your investigations, and analysis. Do you accept the job?

Yes, we think the subject matter would be something worthwhile in pursuing. It has always been a field of study that has been skirted around forever, and candidly, not given much attention. So, we will accept the job with enthusiasm and will depart immediately and try to find a perfect candidate for our study. We will search high and low in our pursuit of understanding.

A while later the research team has concluded its search.

Looking over the whole world we think we have finally found a subject to examine, probe and explore all his qualifications as to being, and what makes him, a common man. We look in.

It was finally morning and everyone was waking up. Well, some were waking up, others had gone to their last sleep in. It wasn't as good a night as say a fancy hotel might offer. The accommodations were at best adequate enough and it did offer a roof over your head, if you can call a tent a roof. The winter was especially cold, but of course, any winter is cold if you live outdoors.

This one particular fellow who we have picked out of this menagerie of men who, as a whole, from the lot of them is let's say average. That is what we are looking for. We didn't want the dredges of society nor the highly educated participants. But an average kind of Joe. One like the boy next door. Your friend or brother or cousin. Just a pick from an average litter. Nothing special about him, nothing that stands out.

We just want to spend a day with an average person, in this case, a soldier, to see what goes on in his head. See what he does, where he goes and what matters most to him. To see what makes him tick.

As we look in on him, we find he is writing a letter to someone. It doesn't matter who it is at this time as we are just seeing what is going on in his world.

Let's look over his shoulder an see what it is he is writing.

His letter starts!

Some days it just doesn't pay to get out of bed. Like this morning, here I was all snug as a bug in a rug in my tent when some jerk thought it would be a good idea to drop a bomb on it. Lucky for me it hit three tents over.

Well, that just ruined my morning. I was hoping to sleep in. It was still 30 degrees outside and just starting to get light. No rest for the little guy. Everybody got all upset and started yelling and carrying on like it was a big deal. I thought so what! You lived, so what's the beef? The guys in the tent it landed on, now they had something to bitch about. That is, if they could have. Not so much anymore, you see my point?

I had to get up because I couldn't sleep anymore anyway, seeing as it was just too noisy and we were told we had to move to another area. Somebody out there had our location down pretty darn good and who knew when the next barrage was coming.

I saw the logic in that and figured why not. The ground I had pitched the tent on was not very flat anyway and something kept sticking me from underneath. So, I was wanting to move anyway.

I was thinking! So, this is what it is like to be homeless? Every time you settle in someplace, get yourself a nice cozy spot and fix it up just right, someone comes along and starts pushing you out. You got to go. You can't stay here. You need to look for greener pastures.

That looking for greener pastures would be nice about now. It is nothing but snow and ice around here. The nice thing about the homeless as I see it is that they can move wherever and whenever they want to. I have to go where I am told to go. At least for now.

My enlistment is almost done. I will be coming home soon. So, I am just chilling for now, literally chilling right now, it's so darn cold. But seriously, things don't bother me as much anymore as they once did. I guess it's because I'm a short-timer. You know almost out. A short-timer!

I have watched a lot of guys getting to be short-timers, packing their gear and shipping out. Going to that elusive place called home. I wonder sometimes if that is really a place or just a figment of my imagination. Maybe when they leave, they just disappear into thin air. I guess I'll find out when my turn comes. They never write me and say everything is great, just nothing at all! They just forget all about us dumb suckers still in the service, no need to worry about us anymore. They're home, right?

It has been a long hard road in the service. Always doing my duty for God and Country. I just wished it paid better. Maybe when I'm finally out I can find a job somewhere warm. In Florida perhaps. I never want to feel this cold ever again. Some of the guys have lost toes to the cold. That would just suck. Is it worth that just to get out of the service? I wonder sometimes if they let that happen deliberately just so they can get out? OK, I'll close for now. I will write more later. I need to post this now. Happy times.

Well, well, it seems John is a little disappointed in the way his military career has been going. Are we sensing a little animosity or resentment toward his fellows for leaving him to continue on?

No! He really wishes them the best. He is just a normal average guy that is feeling the normal average emotions of watching day after day, the leaving of his friends; his comrades in arms, his confidants. This would make anyone show some semblance of self-pity to his predicament.

No, he absolutely wants those who have left before him to attain the best life has to offer. With dreams fulfilled and wishes complete and love within their hearts or something along those lines anyway. Maybe throwing in a couple of good-looking babes wouldn't hurt either.

We seem to have forgotten for a moment our objective of keeping up with John so without further ado we return.

We find the outfit has gotten their gear together and are ready to head out to parts unknown. Well somebody knows where they are going but just never seems to inform the enlisted ones of anything. Falling back on the essential need to know basis is always their excuse. Not that it matters much. One place is usually like the rest, just as bad as the last!

We catch up with John marching in single file through the woods always muttering to himself about everything that comes to mind. And there seems to always be something to mutter about. So, you could say John likes to mutter to himself, which I think we have covered thoroughly enough already.

Maybe we should listen in and see what the average man mutters about? Maybe it is concerning world affairs, the price of beef and how it has gone sky high recently, or maybe, it is the latest in the ranking of his favorite ball team. Let's listen to his mind in action.

“Bummer, John's mind said. Why did we have to leave so quickly this morning? I mean what possible difference does a couple of hours make. We could have gotten some of the wood just lying around everywhere and built such a warm and cozy fire!

“I got this nice rabbit I snared last night and would love to cook it before it spoils. I just hope it doesn’t have any diseases or worms.

“I know we can’t build a fire, yea, yea, I know. That would give away our position and all hell would break out. But man what a few glorious moments of pure warm air and hot toasty toes would do for morale. “The smell of burning shoe leather from feet to close to the fire, your fingers thawing out from days of cold numbing stiffness. And your ears, man, just to be able to feel them again would be wonderful.

“Dang it, there he goes again. I really do pity that guy in front of me. He obviously got a bad C-Ration. Sometimes you get a bad can and if you don’t smell it good and sample it right you just might get what this poor shmuck has got. A bad case of the runs and gas galore. I wouldn’t wish that on anybody.

Wait a minute, maybe I should take that back. There are a couple I could think of to give this too.

“But I mean really! Why did I have to be the one stuck behind him. I know I have to keep close and stay in line because there are reportedly land mines in the area and we all have to follow in the last guys' footsteps or risk, well you know. But hells bells how it smells. Just a one-man walking fart-factory. And then we all have to stop and wait till he craps every few minutes, like the smell of his farts weren’t bad enough. This is not turning out to be one of my favorite days.

“Yea, there are a couple of people I would love to send a bad can of rations to. My wife and my best friend. My wife who is as cold and heartless as the ground I woke up on this morning, just sent me a Dear John Letter. No pun intended, thank you very much.

“She said she and my Best Friend have hooked up and have been doing the toe-curling boo-gey’. The twice around the park, bark. The roll in the hay twice a day, while cooking a filet. Well, I got news for her. If he takes her off my hands, he truly would be My Best Friend!”

Maybe we should give John a little space for a while. He seems to be going through some hard times, more than usual even for him.

After a while, everyone had gotten into a quiet slow-moving train of bodies. Each mimicking the other. Everyone thinking their own thoughts. John was finally reconciled to his fate of being behind the sick fellow and accepted his bad fortune as just part of the job. How brave he is.

Just as we are getting back into his head for more reporting of his thinking.

BOOM! "What the hell was that?" John said as he and everybody else hit the ground and covered. John peeked up from his prone position and saw the blast had come from the front of the line. So that was it he said to himself. Another guy that didn't know how to properly use a metal detector. Moving too fast, no doubt. Taking too big a step and not completely covering the area before moving up. That mistake won't happen again, not by him. Just doesn't pay to get in a hurry.

I guess it's time to take a break and pick another who's on first replacement. John thought. Man, I hope it's not me. They know I am set to rotate out soon. I kind of feel a little guilty thinking this way, but having lived through all the hell up till now, and with just a week to go? Nope, it looks like they got a volunteer. I just love volunteers.

I remember my brother who as a marine went out of his way to emphasize one vital lesson to his little brother just joining up.

He said to me, "whatever you do, don't volunteer for anything."

I took that piece of advice and ran with it. I recall the first time the Drill Sargent asked for volunteers to drive some vehicles. Man, the hands that went up. Many hands went up, but not mine. The Drill Sargent said "OK, all you volunteers step forward."

They all believed they were going to get out of our usual regimen and drive a shiny new jeep for someone. Not going to happen. Instead, he told each and every one of them to report to supply and secure a push mower and start mowing the grass all over the area. They mowed till midnight. Thank you, brother.

Wasn't that enlightening. John has some common sense after all it seems. What more is this character hiding. Maybe he's not the average guy we had first thought. He just might have some gray matter between his ears. That could be why he has received a few decorations, citations and awards. We thought he just got lucky.

It seems we're back in line again. This time John found a different guy to follow. Yes sir, maybe he is smarter than we had first given him credit.

A little later the company stopped to take another rest period. Packing all that gear turned it into more of a drop-in-place moment. But John, our average guy had to pee. So, taking advantage of the respite, he and another lug went to the edge of the forest and started doing their business. Let's listen in. You never know when average guys will talk.

John, standing and relieving himself next to the lug said "man, I almost didn't make it. That was too long a wait between breaks, I must have drunk too much water this morning." The man next to him started to say something and, CRACK, a shot rang out and the guys' head just exploded.

John hit the ground for the second time that day. He looked around quickly trying to pinpoint the location of where the shot came from. It was across the field he told himself. The gunshot came from the other side of this field. “Sniper,” he yelled to the company.

I hate snipers, John was thinking. You never know when they are going to get you. Damn, you can’t even take a pee anymore without worrying about this----. Looking at the guy next to him, he couldn’t finish his thought.

Luck of the draw John thought. Sometimes he wondered why another guy gets it and not him. Not that he wasn’t grateful, he definitely was.

So, as we contemplate his reflections, it seems the average man just accepts his lot in life and hopes all will work out in his favor in the long run. Just luck of the draw.

John contemplated, I wonder what these snipers think about when they see a person in their sights and know they are going to snuff them. Just say it’s your turn, and pull the trigger? No conscience, no feeling of fair play, no wondering if the guy they’re doing has a family! Do they care?

John understood the ways of war as he considered their options and resigned himself to what would happen next. We are going to try and hunt this guy down. Sometimes we get lucky, most of the time we just get more dead soldiers! This one was personal for some reason. It really shook him to watch the guy's head next to him just explode. He had seen plenty of dying. But this was to close and too graphic. This one will haunt him for a long time.

John was thinking, this is why soldiers don't come home and talk about what happened to them in the war. Why they only talk to other soldiers on the few times they do talk. Only another fellow soldier would get it, and understand what he was truly saying. John knew that civilians could never grasp the horror of that moment. It was not like the movies. This you could see, touch, smell and feel.

The worst part of it was that you would remember it all, at any moment, at the most, inopportune times. Not even wanting it to, it was just there in a flash. Something just triggers it. Reality was a bitch, John thought.

We, the ones looking into John's thoughts are troubled by what he has just thought. It never occurred to us before at the impact on a person such as he is having to deal with the horrors of war. It never entered our minds that the soldier standing here was not capable of just taking what came and upon returning to civilian life could not just forget it all and go on with his life. Being of those who have never had to deal with these tragic moments it is hard to grasp the emotions that must be running rampant in John's brain.

How can society not help these men when they return, expecting them to go about their business with these things haunting them.

This sheds a new light on who John really is. What a gifted man he is that can hold up to these moments he has to live with, fought through, day after day, and retain any semblance of sanity. A truly remarkable human being. We who have listened, salute you for your courage and devotion to your duty. We wonder if those amongst us could do the same and retain our sanity as well.

But enough of this retrospect for we have a job, as John does also, to learn what we can from an average man.

So, back to the moment. We see John and several fellow soldiers heading out to, hopefully, track down this killer of men, and seek justice for his fallen comrade in arms, and also praying they all come back alive. After all, this is not the game, we first envisioned. This is reality. This is war.

John speaking quietly to the team accompanying him said," keep your eyes and ears open and your mouths shut. Use hand signals when necessary. Let's get this guy and come back safe."

We watch as the team fanes out and covers a large area. Walking toward the last known location of the sniper. John had done these jobs before. It was not a pleasant job but somebody had to do it. As we listen to his thoughts, we are allowed to hear, the plan. It is a good one. One that sometimes worked. Sometimes? Well, we will see.

John hears the CRACK of another shot being fired. Another soldier dies. Then another CRACK, another shot fired. But this time from another location. Then you hear a paced out three rounds fired, the all-clear signal.

John stands now. "OK, he said out loud. We got him. Let's report back."

We who watch, are aware of the plan. It did work, after all, this time.

The plan John had set up was for him and a small group to go fishing. That is to try and get the sniper to show himself or find him, whichever came first. Then snipers from Johns' company would wait and if possible, try to pinpoint the enemy sniper before any real damage could be done and take him out. It usually meant one or more casualties more but it had to be done or that sniper would just keep picking the company's men off one at a time.

We now can conclude war seems to be a numbers game. Whoever is left standing in the end wins! They are the ones who get to write the history books about what happened. Who was the most just in their cause!

We seem to have been reflecting again about the situations we are witnessing more often lately. So, let's once again get back to our mission.

John is moving along with the company at a leisurely, pace. Just covering ground. Trying to make it to the next rendezvous point before dark. Everyone is pleased and relieved they had gotten the sniper.

John's thoughts settled into reminiscing about his time in the Fire Department before he joined the fight. Let's listen in.

Mark, it's been a long time since I have thought about you. Remember how we used to go on double dates to the drive-in. I still can't remember what movies we went to see, too busy in the kissing department.

Then on a dare, we joined the volunteer fire department. You took to that like a duck to water. Man, that got intense once in a while.

I remember one occasion we were called to a house fire and found some kids trapped in the second-floor bedroom. You didn't even hesitate you just ran for the ladder and after placing it, you climbed up that ladder and brought down three little kids from their burning house.

We all watched as you crawled into the window and came out with each kid, how you kept going back in until you thought there were known left to save.

Then the mother yelled that one of the kids was not there. You climbed back up and disappeared into the smoke-filled room. We waited for a long time. We had just about given up on you when you popped your head out and yelled, "it's ok, I got her." The little girl had been so scared she had hidden in the closet. What a hero you were that day. You always took the risks that others shied from.

I also remember how you pulled that lady from her burning car. It was crazy how you just ran up to it and broke the window out and pulled her through it just before the whole thing exploded in flames. What a guy.

I sadly remember also your last attempt to do your job faithfully. The Fire Captain said someone needed to get on the roof and hack a hole through it so we could get a hose into the interior of the building. You didn't even hesitate. You just climbed up that ladder, got on the roof, and started hacking away.

Maybe if we had gotten proper training, we could have known of the possible danger that the situation entailed and been more cautious in our approach to it.

I will never forget the moment you got the hole open and just fell through it. The fire had obviously eaten away at the underside without us knowing it. And the whole thing just caved in. As you fell in, the flames rose from the hole. We knew there was no hope.

Yea, you were always the one I looked up to. The one I wanted to pattern my life from. You were the best of the best. I guess you're the main reason I joined up. I wanted to carry on your legacy of honor and bravery and service. I sure do miss you.

We are very touched by what we have just heard. John is really a nice guy. He values friendships and holds to a high standard of morals. He seems to be someone who you would be proud to call a friend. Some woman is going to be lucky to have him as a husband. He appears to value all the decent parts of humanity.

Once again, we start listening in on John's thoughts. He is wondering when someone is coming to take him for processing out of the service. He should be heading the other way by now. Not going toward the front lines. This can't be good he is thinking. They are going to put me into battle just before I am set to go home? Man, that's a bum deal. That will read just fine on my tombstone. Here lies John. Died on his last day of service. Somebody screwed up his paperwork.

It looks like the company has made it to the Rendezvous Point. Time to set up camp again and wait for the next continual set of orders to move out to whatever hell hole the brass can figure out to send them next.

John has settled into his tent and is writing another letter. We feel kind of uncomfortable now. Having gotten to know him so intimately in looking over his shoulder, it is like now we are intruding into his privacy. We feel guilty. But a job is a job.

His letter says:

Mamma: I want you to know that I love you. I know it has been hard without my brother and me being there to take care of you. But hopefully, the money we send is helping out. I want to apologize for all the different problems I caused you growing up. I realize I was a handful. But this war, it was just something I had to help out with. I just could not let that tyrant come into our country and do to it what he was doing over here. It is better to keep the fight here than at our home.

I guess you were right about my wife. You always told me I should have married Barbara. I should have listened. Maybe when I get back, if she is still single?

I am supposed to ship out of here soon. I practically have my discharge in my hand. The guys are all calling me a short-timer. I love that name now.

I sure do miss you. And I sure do miss being home. Not that being here wasn't great. All the best four-star accommodations, fine cuisine, wine, women and song. Not to mention the best friends a guy could ask for. All of us just sitting around the lounge talking about all the fun we're having and how much we're going to miss it all. It almost makes you want to re-enlist. I said ALMOST.

So, take heart and say a prayer for big brother and me. And I will see you soon. Love you. Your son, John.

We as the ones taking notes on the average man soldier are genuinely moved by John's devotion and caring for his family. A true American through and through. And such a swell guy. We hope he finds this Barbara unmarried. He deserves a break.

Well, it has been a long day and we have seen and heard much. We have learned that the common man is really not so common. He is almost everybody. The common man is in the majority. He is not of the few, he is of the many. He is not special or unique. He is pretty much like most everyone else. We finally grasp why he is called the common man.

He is not of the unique few individuals who attain power, riches, and fame. Those would not be common at all. But neither did we think the common man to be so plentiful.

He is the everyday run of the mill guy you would meet on any corner; in any bar, in any home, and in any Church. He makes your cars; he delivers your mail, he is your Police, your Firemen, and of course your Soldiers fighting your war.

So, we end the day of looking at our random pick into what makes up a common man and thank him secretly, as he never knew we were there, and bid a fond farewell.

And if you have a need to find out what happened to John from this point on. Sorry, we are just doing our job and have no clue what will transpire after this moment.

If we looked farther, we would not be following our directive by looking into John's destiny. That would be a different report altogether. And we weren't paid for that service.

But we can hope that life deals him a good hand and would see him home safely.

BIOGRAPHY

David Henley has spent a lifetime writing a variety of personal and topical song lyrics, poems and diverse thoughts about life and love themes. He encompasses a myriad of situations, experiences and encounters from everyday lives everyone can relate to in a common man style verse.

In his debut book {POEMS, LYRICS AND DIVERSE THOUGHTS} he imparts a special moment in time, that everyone can find within themselves which should awaken a memory they have at one time lived. The lyrics in this book are from the songs he has written. The Poems and Diverse Thoughts are a culmination of his experiences from his own life as well as many others.

{THE LAST RIDE IS FREE} Is his first thriller fantasy novel about three people and their adventures into the world of criminals and honest society. A journey from the dark side of humanity toward more enlightened soul-searching encounters.

{THE LAST RIDE IS FREE PART TWO} is his soon to be released continuation of a second fantasy thriller novel in the series about the Malone family. It is packed with the same nonstop action as the first book. It has also brought the son into the fold as an agent working alongside his parents, Mario and Julie.

{A DAY IN THE LIFE OF SARGENT SMITH} is a short story about an unknown group of entities searching for what makes a common man different from all others. Just a fantasy action thriller looking into a subject long ignored.

In addition to his writings, he has also worked on ideas for a gravity-powered water generator, which was for a while, first place on a popular search engine. Search GRAVITY POWERED WATER GENERATOR, with BRUTUS as his moniker. He has also worked on a rotating water tub generator and an assisted magnet generator. All in the hopes to help achieve, and give to the world, a free energy device for all to use.

He has also hand-built many treasure chest trunks, in many styles, including the very popular pirates' treasure chest, round top model.

Made in the USA
Middletown, DE
25 October 2024

63123242R00020